Easy

Contents

written by Rachel Walker

Cheese is tasty food that is good for you. This is an easy way you can make cheese at home.

To make cheese you will need:
Milk   Vinegar
Salt   Spoons
Pan or pot   Bowl
Cheesecloth

First, you need to pour one cup of milk into the pot. Turn on the heat, and keep stirring the milk until you see bubbles coming up.

Watch out!   It will be very hot.

vinegar

Turn off the heat, and add two teaspoons of vinegar to the hot milk.

lumps

Keep stirring, and watch the mixture begin to turn lumpy. This is called curds and whey.

7

curds and whey

The curds are the lumps, and the whey looks like water. Leave this mixture to keep warm on the stove for five or ten minutes.

cheesecloth

Put a clean piece of cheesecloth over a bowl. Pour the curds and whey slowly onto the cloth, and then squeeze out the water.

Don't forget to add a pinch of salt to the curds. You could add some herbs or spices if you want to make it more tasty!

10

herbs and spices

Then squeeze all the water out again, and press the curds into a round shape like a ball.

Now you have made homemade cheese. How delicious! You can keep your ball of cheese in the refrigerator.

It tastes nice spread on bread or crackers, or you can eat it with some fruit or salad.

People have been making cheese at home for a long, long time.

pizza

They add it to food they cook,
like pizza and muffins and pasta.

Making cheese at home is fun to do if you use this easy recipe. Enjoy your easy cheese!